EARL'S OWN DAKOTA ODYSSEY

A WEST RIVER STORY
by Bruce Roseland

Copyright © Bruce Roseland 2024. No part of this book may be reproduced or distributed in any form or by any means, or stored in a data base or retrieval system, without written permission from the author. All rights, including electronic, are reserved by the author.

First edition 2024.

Cover image by Doris Symens-Armstrong. Untitled. Oil on gallery wrapped canvas, 14"×11".
Final image by Doris Symens-Armstrong. Untitled. Pen and ink, 3"×4".

Scurfpea Publishing
P.O. Box 46
Sioux Falls, SD 57101
scurfpeapublishing.com
editor@scurfpeapublishing.com

Contents

Introduction.................................... v
Earl begins 1
Found skills.................................... 3
Earl on a roll 5
Earl on ice 7
Dedicated occupation 9
Everyday West River 11
Day job.. 13
Some have a plan 17
Some just got fate 19
There's got to be a morning after........... 21
Facts of life 23
Step out the back, hop on a truck – Earl....... 25
Beyond the Cheyenne breaks................. 27
Free range Earl.............................. 29
Working cattle............................... 31
Earl's post-graduate education............... 35
Twenty years on a roll 37
Oh, what a night............................ 39
How legends are made 41
Consequences 45
Pearls of insight 47
Roll of the dice, or red ain't always the answer.. 49

Trouble begins, this time	53
Trouble in need	55
Trouble resolved	57
Dead ends	59
Earl makes a choice	63
Rambling on not taken	65
Hero Earl	67
Tender mercies	69
About the author	73

Introduction

Earl's Own Dakota Odyssey started from a chance occurrence with "Earl." I was driving into late afternoon sun on a West River, South Dakota, road: State Highway 34. It was mid-February, on a snow-covered prairie. I was late for an important medical appointment in Rapid City.

I was practically blinded by the snow glare. The road was snow-packed and ice-covered, to boot. Suddenly from my side vision, I became aware of a fellow waving his arms wildly next to a slid-into-the-ditch pickup. He was in need of help. I just couldn't leave a fellow traveler stranded like that on a long stretch of sparsely-used West River highway.

I backed up, and this wizened, skinny guy, nearly toothless, who could have been 40 going on 70, smoking a camel straight, came tapping on my window. He asked if I had a tow rope to pull him out. He had only a short chain, which turned out to be about five feet in length. I did have a tow strap, brand new. So, I walked down into the ditch, through the knee-deep snow and attached it to his chain.

The pickup he was driving was old, black and dented. The front window was caved inward, still intact except for a softball size hole in the middle, stuffed with a red bandana. Judging by the tire tracks leading from the road, the windshield hole happened elsewhere.

I did pull him out of the ditch. It was a bit touch-and-go, since he gunned his engine and we almost sling-shotted into an oncoming semi. I retrieved my tow strap. He thanked me and was on his way. Never once did he express any concern for his misfortune, but was positive, practically cheerful. I got the feeling this was just another day in his life. I didn't ask for his name or where he hailed from or was going. He didn't volunteer any info or ask any of me.

Continuing my own drive, I got to thinking. Obviously, there was a story here. That's how the first chapter got written. So…what happened to this fellow before the ditch? That was another chapter. What happens to this fellow after the snowy ditch mishap, was an additional chapter. I only had hope he had a good place to land. Surely, he needed that.

About eight months later, as I was driving West past the Cheyenne River, just west of the river's cedar breaks, Earl came to sit down beside me. No, not a real Earl, but the composite voices of the number of Earls I've met throughout my life. The name Earl just kind of fit. Maybe a Gus, but no, he was an Earl.

Earl told me his life story, in many ways a tough story, but in many ways, he lived the sort of life he chose. A lot of it wasn't so bad. I put down later what Earl told me, pretty much verbatim, and wrote some more chapters of Earl's life.

When I crossed the Cheyenne River going West for the next couple months, Earl would tell me more of his life. I came to realize this was, in effect, an odyssey – a Dakota odyssey.

I've known some Earls in my life. Perhaps you, too, have known a few. I only have the best wishes for them all. They are the folks who live their lives with the cards life has dealt them and make the best of it.

Wherever you are, Earl, I hope you've got a long-neck beer in your hand and a warm roof over your head.

Bruce Roseland
Poet Laureate of South Dakota

Earl begins

Earl was born on a cold November morning,
the kind that has icicles, a foot of snow
and grows into what folks refer to as a hard winter,
pegging the year of his birth as a rough one.

There he grew up, on the wrong side of the tracks
of a small Dakota town, where the railways
were pulled up about as soon
as they were laid down,
not that they ever made much difference.

His father had drifted off like an autumn tumbleweed,
leaving no tracks, and for Earl, no memories.
His mother made do on black and white TV,
Schlitz and welfare.
"One and done," she told everyone,
with a nod at Earl.

So, Earl made do, too,
watching older men take care of their idle time,
drinking beer, clinking pool balls
under neon Hamm's signs,
listening to them talk "girls."
The early childhood education that took hold
in this one room pool hall school,
delivered a hitting, frequently missing,
alternative set of learning.

High school in a nearby slightly bigger town
was a blur, sitting in the back of class,
laughing at others' sass, nodding off,
waiting for lunch and four years ticking by,
ending with an unsigned diploma
and a quick handshake.

Walking across the auditorium's stage
was Earl's one and only achievement,
other than senior year 3rd string bench warmer
on a losing football team.

Hard to belong where there is no belonging,
just relief at being released,
free at last on a warm spring day,
not a clue as to what to do,
and no skills to do it with.

The open road was a big blank page.
Like a tumbleweed, Earl rolled out of town.

Found skills

In cow country, jobs center around
sets of four hooves or wheels,
and they better be in motion.

In Earl's case, the first spring
following his shove out on his own,
he found rodeo, although
he had not a horse, saddle or riggings,
but he could straddle the top rail,
yell with the best, once tried a rank bull
and found once was enough.

Occasional clowning, with borrowed
red lipstick for a face, his clothes
already raggedy, provided some pay.
Adrenalin and youth kept him
a few inches ahead of certain death
in the chase for the fence,
saving Earl's butt and the left behind
spilt-from-his-ride cowboy
on the arena's ground.

As the cowboy limped off,
the announcer's voice boomed out,
"Don't worry folks, that cowboy is A-OK,"
which is what the announcer said after every ride,
no matter what shape that cowboy was in.
Concern for the clowns, not so much.

Not a great way to make a wage,
but there were beers afterwards
sitting on tailgates
and buckle bunnies that just might
consider him a consolation prize,

after those with the winnings
walked off with the cutest cowgirls.

Usually, if he got lucky,
Earl ended up with a bed on top
of square bales to sleep on by his lonely
and a ride to the next rodeo event.
This was the beginning of learning
the trade of saddle bum.

Earl on a roll

Summer flew by with Earl's newfound friends.
There was always a way to the next town.
In a pinch, he used his thumb.
In a pinch for money, he used card poker tricks
from his childhood pool hall days,
careful from whom he took wins.

Like a summer breeze,
all summer he floated
across the Dakota plains,
a butterfly he felt like at times,
clowning through rodeos in a beer haze,
counting evening stars
wherever he ended up that night.

All the fellows he met had handles for names,
Red from Wall, Burt from Buffalo,
Shorty from Somewhere,
Slim, because he was not.
The girls were all known by their first names.
They stayed behind while the boys moved on.
Seemed like a reasonable game.

One night Earl's luck ran out
when caught with an ace too many
and a dollar short, ducked a punch
that landed instead on a mean, mean drunk,
who took offense at having his drink spilled
and round-housed the first face he could hit.

These ruckuses at the midnight hour
have a way of spreading
from one tipsy cowboy to the next,
and soon the law was called in.

Earl just didn't have the good sense to crawl off
or meekly go into the black and white
with the bright red and blue lights.
He ran to the first vehicle he could find,
beginning the chase.

Earl on ice

"What do you have to say for yourself?"
asked the judge of Earl,
after the citation of various
petty misdemeanors,
mainly consisting of almost successfully
evading arrest, by backroads, sideroads,
and absolutely no roads
that any sane pursuing deputies
would want to go down.

*Seemed logical not to stop
when you had no license*,
thought Earl, as he stood before
a stern looking judge.

Several still steaming deputies
sat in the courtroom's front row,
their county-issue cars dented,
exhaust pipes torn off.

But Earl had a sense of humor,
even wit at times. There was a pause
in court, perhaps even a hush,
as his eyes lit up.

Looking straight at the judge,
a smile upon his hungover face,
Earl brightly said, *Make joke?!*
Wrong time for wit, as the judge's gavel
came down, "90 days."
That judge has no sense of humor,
thought Earl.

Dedicated occupation

Inside every cowboy bar early afternoon,
or outside on wooden benches on hot days,
sit a few, slouched back on haunches,
nursing a beer grown warm,
working on a chew, watching, talking slowly
about what might be new.

Could be an old pickup that changed hands,
could be a horse for sale, although none among them
had pasture or a lot they could rent to keep one.
Sometimes the talk turned to a job
with good pay, but a bit too far to consider.

Best yet, when the talk turns to a new lady
in town with a job, who cuts quite a sight
and hasn't yet got herself a man.

Then the debate begins as to who among
this small crowd of cowboy tramps
has more merit, who would be the one
she deserves for company.

The day goes by, the lights go on.
Those with jobs pull up for happy hour,
and this little crowd sees what the night brings.

Earl fitted to this scene early on
like a hand in a glove,
like a man who will never own a wedding ring.

The trick was to find a lady to support you
in suitable style.
If you're dedicated, a man can make a run off this,
get himself a good 20 years.

Everyday West River

Western, in the Dakotas, means
you grew up West of the Missouri River
that cuts the states into two bites,
West and East.
The West has cowboy hats for shade,
high boots for comfy, practical rattlesnake gear.

Pickup trucks go down sparsely traveled
West River roads
where there's at least one cow, if not a couple hundred,
on either side.

Not everyone here owns cows,
but seems like most have access to a horse or five
tucked away on gramp's old ranch
or standing, stomping their feet
in grass paddocks chewed to the ground
with a lone half-eaten hay bale in a ring feeder
somewhere on outskirts of small towns,
or alongside faded trailer houses
sitting alone on dusty roads.

Here, too, are 30-year-old 3/4-ton Fords
with dents and cracks running along salt-rusted sides,
8 MPG rigs that pull even-more-worn-out goosenecks,
with balding low tires, maybe, ready to roll.

The rules of this semi-arid land are simple.
Everyone's paycheck starts in the belly of a cow.
Rain makes grass, grass makes cows,
cows make calves, calves go to the sales barn,
paying bills from the bank, from the feed store, or
to the liquor store, not always in that order.
No rain, no paycheck.

Roughly speaking, out of five years,
one is wet, one is God-awful dry.
The other three years slip in between,
depending if hail or grasshoppers hit.
These are facts of life in the Western bite.

Most folks, on most years, pull down the brim
of their hats, squint into the sun,
hoping the next day and year will be better,
having learned it's not polite to whine,
except maybe about the weather.

This is a land of pride,
a land to keep a stiff upper lip
and a chew of Copenhagen in the bottom one,
where the full cut of character can result in
scoundrel or legend; frequently hard to tell
which has the last say.

What you see is what you got,
plenty of wide-open space
and few who will tell a body you can't,
well . . . anything.

This kind of country is where the likes of Earl
find room for freedom to do as they please,
as long as expectations are kept low.

Day job

In the Dakotas, cowboys don't take welfare,
even though their baby mamas might,
between jobs.

Getting desperate for something to get him by,
preferably not requiring heavy lifting
or deep thinking, Earl needed at least a part-time job.

Earl's skills as a ladies' man
couldn't get beyond hello, definitely not his strongest suit.
He remembered sitting at the bar
with a senior (old, that is) cowboy. "Son, a good horse
is like a good woman. Both of 'em hard to find
and neither of 'em come cheap.
I should know, I've had a few of both."
Earl believed the man, but wasn't sure about all he meant.

Earl's attempts at earning
a few dollars in card games resulted
in pockets stuffed full of I.O.U.s from bar crowd players
even broker than him.

So, Earl sought employment.
The livestock auction barn four blocks from the bar
was an easy walk.

Earl showed up on a busy day, hired on,
shooing skittery calves and testy bulls to numbered corrals,
slipping their papers under mouse trap snaps,
closing gates, and repeat.

With one shuffling boot step on sloppy concrete
and then the next, he walked up the barn's alleys,
pushing cattle early mornings, when the rush
of semis and trailers pulled in, backing up,
with clank and clatter of steel tailgates
disgorging slipping, sliding, stampeding bovines
between two guys making a head count.

Three slips of paper, one for Earl to stick underneath
the pen's mouse trap, one to the driver
and the other back to the sale barn office,
is the how of how hundreds of thousands
of dollars got tracked.

After each bunch runs through the inside auction ring,
with the sing-song auctioneer calling out
the ups and downs of bids,
these lots of cattle are sold to the highest bidder,
buyers marking their buy cards,
sitting on wooden bleachers above the ring.

Earl shook the BBs in his rattle-paddle,
scooting the rear-enders
back through alleys to designated pens,
where later they would be loaded out,
shipped down highways to their fate.

Made sense to Earl.
Cattle come in, cattle go out,
and at day's end, a paycheck.
For himself and the other sale barn hands,
there were two sale days a week,
a few hours watering and scraping runways
on off days, the weekends, free.
Just enough to get by.

Earl had found new friends,
a couple of which had an old RV on the edge
of town that, somehow, had a couch
that fit him good after the after-work beers.

Some have a plan

Saturday nite, always special,
those moments, hours to get away with indulgences,
a time out from the usual.
Even more so when the Fourth of July rodeo
lands on a weekend.

The real action, fun, excitement happens
not in the bleachers, but back of the chutes,
back where the RVs are parked
in rows like streets, back where the horses
are tied to the trailer gates, quietly stomping,
right to left foot, tails swishing flies,
back where the beer keg sits flowing free,
the plastic 16 oz. cups wait, stacked in towers,
to be filled up, sipped and gulped by
cowboys, cowgirls, hangers-on around
the driftwood campfire, where a makeshift
community of boots and hats swap stories,
truth and lies, the boys and girls
giving each other an appraising eye.

The end-of-the-rodeo twenty-minute fireworks
had already lit up the star-spangled night sky.
Earl was just settling in comfy-cozy,
on his fifth or sixth filled-to-the-brim alcohol suds.
Almost in a state of philosophical mood,
Earl was feeling good, having found his niche
in the last year, a place to sleep, a means for eats,
all the direct result of a steady paycheck,
courtesy of the local auction barn.

Earl had found an easygoing acceptance
with the downtown bar crowd, where he spent the bulk
of his off-work time and paycheck.
Now and then he bought the toughest hombre walking in
a drink, good for community relations and his health.

Yep, Earl had a feeling of steadiness.
Seemingly, he had found his calling.
But just like a pyramid stack of empty beer cans,
it doesn't take much to upend.

Some just got fate

From the edges of the night,
just outside the campfire's light,
a commotion stirred and then emerged.
Bouncing, shimmering and whooping it up,
a young lady appeared, long black hair
whipping in the night air,
a white cowgirl hat tipped far back,
singing a Mary Chapin Carpenter tune
about what cowgirls do.
Well, they dance real close to you
"Down at the Twist and Shout."

Oh yeah, the little lady was 17 sheets to the wind,
and it looked like all 17 were in a tornado.
Earl could swear there were sparks
flying from her fingertips,
mixing it up with sparks from the campfire.
But oh, oh, oh, how she was dancing around that fire!
Her boots were stamping, legs flashing,
arms windmilling with her imaginary guns popping.

She switched to singing about tequila,
swirling to pretend-shoot the lights out,
when she stumbled.
Earl, being the gentleman he is,
caught her like a falling star.
Looking up at Earl with a face full of pure sweet,
"Fill my glass up? What's your name?
Mine is Sue Zann."

So went the night for Earl, as he joined in dancing
around and around in the campfire light
with the high-spirited dancing lady.
Around Earl's 10th beer, he remembered

being led by a feminine hand, with her other arm
tight around his neck, ruby red lips giggling in his ear,
to a lone RV parked at the end of the row
and then, the foggy memory of doing
what neither should have done.

There's got to be a morning after

All nites end, for both good and bad,
the sun comes up, light shines on all.
From a yip and a start, Earl woke,
through blurry sight, seeing his cowgirl beauty
adjusting her garb. "Holy smokes!
Look at the time!" she exclaimed.
To Earl's bloodshot eyes, she still looked
mighty fine.

"Gonna be hard to explain to Dad
about where I've been, but what the heck,
I'll tell him I met you and you'll vouch
for the night."
At that, Earl saw what might become a complication.
"I gotta find my truck, and vamoose," Sue Zann said,
"but whatcha say,
you'll be my Homecoming date?"
Date? Earl asked himself, *Homecoming?*
College? he asked out loud, *College?*
"Oh, my no!" said Sue Zann. "After this fall's
big football game." *Ah*, said Earl,
and then a longer *ahh...How old are you?*
"Seventeen, going on eighteen," Sue Zann said,
as she bounced out the RV door. "See you soon."

At that moment, Earl had a sudden onset
of the biggest pounding hangover headache
he ever had and an overwhelming, nagging
banging at the back of his head,
beyond a simple impending hint of uneasiness.

Facts of life

With an unsteadiness to his feet,
Earl made his way to the smoldering embers
of last night's fire, and found one of his stockyard buddies
tipping back the keg, getting the last cupful
of foamy dreg. "I see you struck it lucky,"
his buddy quipped. "Might be a problem, though.
Sue Zann is the only daughter
of the biggest ranch man in fifty miles."

So? What's so bad about that? asked Earl.
"Nothing, except stories of ranch hands gone missing
who just looked at her the wrong way."
Just looked at her the wrong way? repeated Earl.
At this, his buddy just shook his head, thinking Earl
might be a little slow this morning.

"Seems her dad is more than just a little protective."
Oh, said Earl. His buddy continued,
in a drawn-out, meaningful tone,
"Her dad's brother is the County Sheriff."
Ohh, said Earl, a little more slowly.
"Yeah. Seems like there are some stories about him, too,"
the buddy added, as he gave the keg one last shake.

The sun was just then rising in all gloriousness
upon the hoof-marked, trampled arena's dirt floor.
Chute-plank corrals peek-a-booed shadows and light
on dawn's dew-slick, tire and foot-traffic-worn grass.
There lay the leftover hotdog, burger wrappers
and crushed, emptied beer cans and dixie cups,
littering the remains of a memorable Fourth of July.

Early morning birds twittered and sang, but all Earl could feel was total, utter, descending blackness of Doom.
Doom, doom, pounding in his hungover, morning after, regret-filled head.

Step out the back, hop on a truck – Earl

There at the back of the rodeo grounds,
Earl choked down his buddy's proffered bitter dregs
from last night's keg.

Weighing his options to what the near future might hold:

1 – Hope for the best, that Sue Zann's father would see
    the humor in how his daughter and Earl met;
2 – Sue Zann's uncle, the Sheriff, would also see
    the humor in how his niece spent the night;
3 – Earl could run like Hell.

Earl chose option #3.

The town was quiet, being the morning of July 5th,
as Earl made his way to the stock yards.
Quiet as a church mouse there, except
for the rustling of a few cows in the back pens.
As luck would have it, Earl found a trucker
pulling out and asked for a ride,
not even asking where, for anywhere, somewhere,
was all he cared.

Luck would have it, the truck was going West.

Earl drifted off into fitful sleep,
dreaming of being pursued by a black pickup truck,
lights flashing, siren wailing, that somehow became
a long black-haired beauty, dancing in firelight,
hands reaching out to him through campfire flames,
suddenly turning into the fires of Hades,
as a man with a star on his shirt, pitchfork in hand,
jabs at Earl's behind as he tries to dodge cattle

stampeding through saleyard alleyways,
man and beasts unable to find a way out.
Then, still dreaming, he stumbled,
scrambling on hands and knees.

Pure panic, heart pounding, Earl woke with a start.
The semi was parked.
His eyes slowly focused on a sign,
GAS EATS BEER.
Earl had an urgent need for two of these.

Several hours later, he found himself
bouncing in the back of a pickup work truck.
His new-found buddies said there's work to be had,
but first, there's a party.
What's not to like about a party? Sounded good to Earl,
giving no thought to the work part.

Beyond the Cheyenne breaks

Next morning, he came to on a bunk house floor –
granted, there was an empty bed
just above his head.

Outside, facing the front door,
was the Cheyenne, the river, that is,
with its cedar-studded breaks back of the bunk house.
Back beyond the breaks, Earl could sense,
and was soon to be part of, thousands and thousands
of acres of short grass plains and a lot of moooos
who needed fences to keep them in.

Earl had a job, apparently,
well maybe, depending on what the foreman had to say,
who with a glance up and down
and a doubtful shake of his head, asked Earl,
"Got a horse?" *Nope*, said Earl.
"Got a saddle, got a rope?" *Nope*, said Earl.
"OK," said the foreman, "Got two hands?" *Yep*, said Earl.
"What's your name?" *Merle*, said Earl.

Knowing he had come to a fork in the road,
and deciding to take it, let anybody tracking him
find, at least, muddy tracks.

With that, Merle, formerly known as Earl,
was sent down the ranch's tens of tens of miles
of barbwire fence lines with a beat-up pickup truck,
a spool of wire in the back, rusty fence staples,
hand post digger and a few wood posts.

In exchange, Earl, now known as Merle,
got a bunk house roof, grub, enough pay
for occasional new-used boots and beer.

Earl free range

The why of why a person stays anchored
in a particular locality may seem random to an outside eye,
but usually has to do with comfort,
or maybe just plain inertia,
like a rock sitting at the tip of a hill.

If Earl was like this rock, he came to appreciate his view.
When working out on the ravine-cut plains,
he could see what was coming for miles around.
He could see dust spiraling upward into the sky
from a dusty road as far as ten miles distant,
having an idea where the traveler was traveling to,
where they probably came from,
and a guess at who.

For some years after landing unceremoniously
at this ranch, Earl nervously watched
those puffs of dust, afraid of those nagging quivers
of unease nipping at the back of a guilty mind.
Over time he learned the patterns of neighbors
and his own ranch's road travelers.

Eventually, he began to relax
and become more like a pair of well-worn work jeans.
No one ever visited the bunk house,
other than the foreman who brought in weekly supplies.
The only excitement was the coming and goings
of mostly seasonal turnover ranch hands.

After the fall calves were weaned,
the mother cows were wintered down in the river breaks,
watering where the river flowed fast.
No longer running fence lines fixing fences,
Earl only needed to break ice on the coldest days.

When snow dusted the ground,
he would load up the cotton cake feeder on a one-ton truck,
stringing out the cows in long, straight lines,
dropping cubes on frozen short grass
where they were gobbled up by hungry bovines,
steam from their breath hanging just above their hides.

Earl then hurried back to a warm bunk house,
which, in time, he came to consider home.
Sparsely furnished, holding only bunk beds,
table and a few chairs, it was where the getting to
became familiar and good,
even though the old color TV was mostly snow,
and the one channel that made its way
to the river bottom was public,
kept on just for background noise.

Time passed, mostly card playing for little or no stakes.
Easy days, the couple hours of work required
were like a vacation, even if it was way better inside
than the cold white world outside.

Working cattle

Spring always came too quickly,
when the work began again in earnest,
a season of caring for, moving around, newborn calves,
tagging those calves to mothers,
moving the new pairs from the wooded, creek-sheltered lots
to more open, but still sheltered, small pastures,
where the little bunches grew to the numbers needed
to make up big summer pastures of thousands of acres
that lay west of the breaks.

When only a few tail-enders were left,
extra help was called in from neighboring ranches.
Real cowboys, twenty or more, chaps, spurs and horses,
would trailer up before dawn, saddle up, ride out,
bring the herds into sprawling corrals not used since fall.

They would let the mamas out one gate
and proceed to rope the babies one by one,
dragging them bawling to a waiting crew.
A couple of guys, one on the front feet,
one on the rear feet, stretched the calves out,
keeping sharp hooves from flying into cowboys' tender parts.
One cowboy clipped budding horns,
another hand turning bulls into steers with a snip, snip.

Vaccine guns flew in and out, touching hide briefly,
giving spring shots, keeping these babies free from disease.
Then comes a slap of a hot iron, a cloud of burning hair,
a legal brand made to deter rustling thieves.
A latex color marker down the calf's back
signified this little critter done, scampering off
not so much worse for wear, back to nursing mom.

Of course, someone with ink and paper
wrote all the doings down.
Serious business, all this,
the beginnings of filling the ranch's bank account.

Earl, over the years, worked his way up
to being the hand in charge of vaccine guns,
instead of his starting out task
of throwing a squirming, kicking calf flat to the ground,
holding rear legs and tail, his own butt firmly in the dirt,
leaning back grasping the calf's legs,
never daring to let go before all done
and risk the wrath of a half dozen grown men
interrupted from an assembly line
of coordinated cowboy work.

Earl was always mindful where the gun needles went,
having once stuck himself in the leg with a dose
of 7-way vaccine and having a big knot swell up,
longtime before it went down.
Better the lesson learned by him than sticking a cowboy
who would never forget or forgive.

Lunch time, and the end of the work day,
home cooked food and cooler beer gave Earl
a sense of fitting in.
These were his kind of folks.

After a day or so of resting up cows, calves, and home crew,
the collected herds were each trailered or slow-walked
to their summer pastures,
turned out to greening grass and pretty prairie flowers.

Earl then would go back to his summer-fall routine,
tending miles and miles of solitary fence lines,
carrying a spool of barbwire, stretchers and cutters,
and drive real slow in a beat-up pickup truck,
whose radio stayed on the same country western station.

Frequently Earl parked his truck way out
where there was no one but cows in the distance,
put his boots up through the passenger side open window,
leaned back his head upon his rolled-up jacket
and took a long snooze.

No worries, no one yammering at him about anything,
just butterflies and the prairie breeze.
What was not to like,
with blue sky, floaty, puffy clouds drifting
slowly west to east,
the smell of western wheat grass and gamma grass
ripening in summer air with a hint of sage.

Some folks might have gotten lonely,
but Earl knew his was a good gig.
He always managed to start up the truck,
finish the fence line repairs and make it back
to the bunk house before dark, then after supper,
step out the front, look at the glittering multitude of stars,
count each night of this as luck.

Earl's post-graduate education

The business side of the ranch
was a mystery to the ranch hands.
No one cared as long as twice a month
the paychecks handed out by the foreman
cleared the local bank.

Most, including Earl, cashed their paychecks
the same day at the same town's one bar,
which also had, conveniently,
a line of western wear. Buy local, good slogan,
and the cowboys did.

Earl's winter routine got a little stirred up
when the foreman, and his horse,
slipped on river ice. Down they went, after which
the foreman had a hitch in his hips' gitch
for a long while.

Earl was pressed into being the foreman's driver
to the occasional local auction barn's sales,
where the foreman would sell a few of the opens
and lame cows, plus bid on small strings
of yearlings to stock the odd and end pastures
that needed grazing down.

The auction barn would send the sellers' checks
or buyers' slips to the absentee owner
to make good. That's how the grandfather did it,
with a handshake, a business style passed on down
to the great-grandson, a privilege earned
until it becomes undone.

Earl, AKA Merle, not wanting to attract attention,
still feeling he needed to stay down low,
stood back in the side stairwell,
watching the ring man scour seats for bids,
listening to the sing-song doings of the auctioneer,
who started on the high side, then dropped down,
working the buyers back to where the sale
would not go a dime higher.
Out the sale ring door the bovines went, sold.

Earl soon learned his boss knew a thing or two,
never buying high, always buying low,
putting together odds and ends that the big buyers
didn't need to make up semi loads,
but that fit real well in the gooseneck trailer
Earl filled at the end of the sale.
Over the course of the winter auctions,
a few yearlings here, a few yearlings there,
those odd pastures ended up full of fine cattle.

By osmosis, this side of the ranch business
sunk in. Earl, at times, felt a hankering
to try his hand, but he had no real money.
He was but a ranch hand.

Still, there was a fascination seeing cattle
and thousands of dollars flowing through
by the nod of a head and a yell
of the auctioneer saying "sold," as the red lights
above the auctioneer's bench
flash cents per pound and number of head.

Earl got, by the way of an unlucky horse fall,
an education of sorts, at last.

Twenty years on a roll

Earl learned his job, cowboying up
and cowboying down
and, once in a while, enjoyed Saturday nite
at the local bar in the nearest little town.

When the jukebox played Mary Chapin Carpenter
songs, he got a little misty, thinking about
a certain long-black-haired dancing lady.
He wondered if things
might not have turned out so bad
if he had taken Option #1,
somehow had stayed clear of Option #2.

Every so often, he would make
a discreet, roundabout inquiry
to a passing stranger about the sheriff
of the county he had so swiftly departed.
Seems like the sheriff had a continuing, long career
and even more so, a reputation for being
unforgivingly hard on law breakers.

A few of these passers-by, with a nervous giggle
and a dart of the eyes, said the sheriff's handle
was "the hanging sheriff." At that,
with an appraising glance at Earl, they would ask
if he ever had a run-in with this sheriff.

At this, Earl would promptly change
the conversation to the weather
or what was the best breed of hunting dogs.

Oh, what a night

One nite, in the midst of getting misty-eyed,
one dang old cowboy kept dropping coins
into Mary Chapin Carpenter's "Twist and Shout."

Earl was fixing to get up and empty his pockets
of change, investing in an hour of Willie Nelson,
when the front door pops open with a gust of wind.
In blew a small gaggle of foxy-looking ladies.
They were not shy. No edging their way in,
instead, more like they came to occupy.

First things first. Drinks ordered to the barkeep.
Not a single, but a line of shot glasses
on the bar counter and then they gave
the male denizens the eye,
since they were the only ladies,
odds were on their side.

This was, to these old boys, a seldom and strange
occurrence, as if a hurricane suddenly materialized
over your favorite fishing pond.
Some of the married men had a sense
of what this may become the makings of,
the gossip wives exchange Sunday mornings
at church. These few started to edge their way
to the exit door.

For others, there was great curiosity
how this rare intrusion of possibilities
dropped into their male sanctuary
of a home away from home, namely,
their local watering hole.

How legends are made

A lot of things in life happen unexpectedly to Earl.
The cutest female, with long black hair sweeping
down her brown leather jacket, knocked back
three shots in a row, chasing them with a tap pour,
stomped her feet on the floor, shouting
"This place needs livening up, let's dance,"
while yanking the nearest cowboy off his stool,
and, Lord be his witness,
just accidentally, this was Earl.

Around the pool table with Earl she twirled,
holding his hand in a death grip,
past the blinking video lottery machines,
picking up her girlfriends as she do-si-doed.
Several more of Earl's ranch hands joined in.

Next tune on the jukebox was country swing.
The black-haired beauty slid into this change of pace,
releasing Earl's now sore hand
and putting her arms around his neck.
From somewhere in his beer-addled memory,
Earl knew he could two-step to this music,
and found his bones doing just that.
It had been a very long time
since he enjoyed anything like this.
He may even have given a hearty little yip.
This night had something familiar.

What's your name? "Jill." *Oh yeah*, as Earl
leaned in, catching a whiff of Chanel #5,
his nose was practically on Jill's neck,
when unbeknownst to Earl, Jill's boyfriend
walked in through the back, having just parked his rig.

Apparently, he was the jealous type.
Earl was spun around, blind-sided with a right.
He went down like a poached deer hit with a .308.
If Earl had good sense, he would have stayed down.
But he was insulted at having been sucker-punched.
Up he staggered, looked at the jealous protector
of Jill's maligned honor, yelling through a busted lip,
You're a Low Down, Dirty Dog,
blindsiding me like that!
Me and the lady was just enjoying a dance.

That's when lover boy hit Earl with a left
with even more heft than the previous right,
cleaving Earl's lower lip in half.
Down he went again,
missing out on the rest of the fight,
as lover boy's friends came streaming into the bar,
and the ranch hands did their best to pitch in.

Tables, chairs and the big mirror back of the bar
became casualties of this night. Who won, who lost,
made lively conversation for years.

If you're traveling through and stop by this establishment,
there's a plaque on the wall that says it all:

> **Next son of a bitch who starts a fight**
> **buys this bar for my asking price,**
> **no discount for anything broken, but first,**
> **I will cut off his manhood with a jagged glass**
> **and throw him and it out with the trash.**

Apparently, the barkeep, who was the owner, didn't have a sense of humor about this particular throwdown.

Consequences

Earl, for the second time, woke up
on the bunkhouse floor, his bunk above his head.
He put a tentative hand to a swollen jaw
and found a few gaps where teeth had been.

He heard through the grapevine, many years later,
Jill had ditched lover boy, gone to college,
married a dentist, had five kids
and was elected president of the local PTA.

Women are too complicated, Earl sighed,
as he found himself staying close to home
on Saturday nites,
nursing long-neck bottles of Budweiser,
watching the fuzzy old color TV trying to bring in
"Austin City Limits."

Pearls of insight

The wind was gusting and moaning
outside the bunkhouse one particularly long
winter night. Earl was shuffling cards.
"Yep," said the one on Earl's left,
"Women can be all right, but they expect three things
from us guys: a kind word or two; a steady job,
as in keeping your nose to the grindstone;
and, no running around, ya gotta be true.
I was pretty good running my mouth
when a good-looking lady came around.
My howdy-doos are like chocolate and candy canes.
I have, let's say, an appreciative eye for a bit of bounce
in a cute skirt. For me, it's hard to stay in one lane.
Unfortunately, all these skirts have a way
of eventually getting wise to my game.
So, I'm good for one of three, 'cause here I am,
playing cards with you guys."

The cowboy on Earl's right had a sad look in his eye.
He quietly said "I had a gorgeous girlfriend, I did.
We traveled the rodeo circuit far and wide.
One rodeo, I tried a nasty old bull,
should've stayed riding broncs.
Damn SOB broke my femur two different ways.
That gorgeous girlfriend of mine gave me a kiss
on the cheek as I was laying on the hospital bed,
saying 'I gotta hit the road. I'm 14th in the Nationals.
There's still a month of barrel racing left.
I'll see ya in Vegas.'
Well, I didn't make Vegas that year
or the next, on account of Mr. Bull.
My rodeoing years were done. In the end,
I think she loved her horse more than she loved me."

Earl dealt the cards all around.
The ranch hand sitting directly across from Earl,
who had grey streaking through hair and beard,
picked up his cards one by one and spoke slowly,
"Boys, all may be fair in love and war,
but maybe love is just for the lucky and strong.
I'll tell you what, I don't miss my Ex.
But I sure as hell miss my kid."

Silence hung heavy on the table
as all four studied their cards.
Breaking the spell, Earl exclaimed,
I got two pair and two ace!
Then there was a scratch of wooden matches,
their handy poker chips exchanged
from one side of the table to the next.

Earl had the bigger pile. They all called it a night.
Later, in bed, he chewed over the wisdom
proclaimed, sorting wheat from chaff.

Roll of the dice, or,
Red ain't always the answer

Still, in his own way, Earl, now known as Merle,
was pretty content.
Blue sky, fresh air, always a cow in the background.
Cows meant he had a job, with one day
leading to the next. A paycheck twice a month.

He got used to the occasional rattlesnake
on his fence-fixing rounds, giving them
a good whump with anything at hand,
preferring to walk around them if he could.
Many of the ranch hands drifted in, drifted out,
but Earl, knowing he had a steady thing, stayed put
through the years, gaining cowboy skills.

He never saw the owner of the ranch,
apparently absentee, the son of the son
of the original one who had pounded
in his homesteading stake on the Cheyenne
and began the long, hard work of building
an empire of cows.

Each generation after this allowed some slippage
of ambition and work ethic.
The blood thinned and the latest genetic edition
had a wandering bent, a taste for high stakes
poker games. Seems only the foreman
had a direct, although infrequent, connection.

One day after this couple of decades,
in which Earl had come more and more to think
of himself as an old hand, round about noon,
when the beans were being reheated,
a small caravan of black Suburbans,
plus two Humvees, pulled up to the bunk house.

A crew of black, pristine Stetson hats
and shiny, dress oxford shoes step out
as the bunk house crew gathered under
the blazing sun.
Earl was befuddled as to what to make
of these clean-shaven,
pressed-dress-shirted, briefcase carrying,
professional type dudes.
Mormons? he thought. *Maybe Jehova Witness?*

First words spoken were "You're fired."

That was news, indeed.
The absentee boss owner had lost it all
in a Las Vegas poker game, namely,
the deed to the ranch. Interestingly, they added,
his wife tossed back her diamond ring,
apparently not wanting a reminder of this fool.
The ring he promptly bet on red at the wheel.

Lost that, too. So, no chance for severance pay.
New owners. Us. New plans. Buffalo.
Lots of buffalo.

No cows. No need of cowboys.
You are all let go. But we will need a few
to drive the Hummer for the Eco Tourists,
for patrons on the Safari Buffalo Tours.
We will bring in our own college-educated guides
to do the talks and walks,
but we will need one or two men to staff
the boutique.

Boutique?! As Merle and the boys looked at each other, the same words fell out, "What the F—K?!"

Thus began the beginning of the next Merle, formerly known as Earl, rambling man.

Trouble begins, this time

Earl woke up cold, on a lumpy couch, head pounding.
With one look, he knew he was in a single-wide
trailer, all alone, no memory of how he got there.
Judging by the light, it was either mid-morning
or mid-afternoon.

Earl found a light jacket, his, with half a pack
of Camel straights in the pocket.
He stumbled outside down the cement block steps,
blinded by the sun shining off early February snow.

All around was empty prairie, except in the far distance,
a butte. In the driveway that led to a dirt track road
was a black 4x4, looking badly beat up and dented,
front windshield caved-in, spider-cracked,
a hole in its middle stuffed with a red bandana.
Earl had never owned a red bandana or a black 4x4.

This is a puzzle, thought Earl.
The driver's door creaked on its hinges, barely shut.
As he got in, the rearview mirror showed a face
unshaven, haggard, but not bloody.
The key was in the ignition.
The only thing to do was fire it up
and see where the dirt road would lead.

Thirty minutes later, he found a blacktop.
Seeing through the shattered windshield
was like looking through a crazed haze
of rainbow reflections.
Not the best ride, still, the engine ran OK – mostly.

All Earl knew was that anywhere else
was better than anything he was leaving behind.
Somewhere nearby had to be the small town
he had landed in last, having shifted from full time
to occasional, part time ranch hand,
bunking with the same sort of fellows as he.

With the sun heading toward setting
and his vehicle pointed west,
the scenery seemed to be getting more familiar
as miles were gained. Suddenly a slippery spot
on the road had him skidding sideways
until he whomped into a snow-covered ditch.
Damn, he thought, as he fished out another smoke.

Trouble in need

An old black, three-quarter ton 4x4 pickup
was stuck, upright, in a snowed-over highway ditch.
From the open driver's side door, a fellow waved wildly
for a new blue pickup to stop, and its driver,
a young man, did, backing up cautiously
until parallel with Earl.

Puffing on a cigarette, looking between 40 and 70,
nearly toothless, on the gaunt side,
Earl came around to the stranger's door.
He said he needed a pull, but he only had a short chain.
Did the driver have a tow rope or strap? The driver did,
and dug a never-used strap out the back of his Ford-150.

The young man hooked the strap onto his back hitch
and walked through deep snow down
to Earl's dented-up truck.
The front windshield was bashed in,
badly cracked, with a melon-sized hole
in the middle plugged by a red bandana.
The rig's been in a roll-over,
but judging from the snow tracks, not here.

Earl's short chain was all of five feet,
light-weight, hitched to the front of his frame.
This, the younger man threaded
through the loop of his tow strap.
Looking up and down the rural highway, he saw no traffic.

"Let's give it a try," the young man said,
"and be sure to go slow."
Took a bit for Earl to get back behind the wheel,
his driver's door was out of whack.
The helpful stranger slipped his gear into 4x4 low,
pulled the slack out slowly.

Earl guns it and skids sideways through snow
for a long way, his tires bald,
until he climbs up and out and to the middle of the road,
just as a semi bears down.

The stranger stays ahead of him,
and somehow, none of them collide.
Earl slows to a stop. Young man retrieves his tow rope,
says goodbye. Earl's in a hurry to vamoose.

The young man could have called the incident in,
but why?
No use having trouble find Earl, when he looked
very able of finding trouble by himself.

Trouble resolved

*Thanks be to the good traveler
who pulled me out of stuck*, thought Earl,
*lucky day and the Lord provides.
Best to keep moving, law starts sniffing around,
trouble starts.*

After a few miles of black top,
Earl hung a right down washboard gravel
that shook some of the windshield glass out.
In his rearview mirror, Earl could see
the law going east on black top,
red and blue lights flashing.
Must be trouble, Earl thought.

He turned left and then right.
This road, he knew.
A double-wide came in sight at a dead end.
Without much thought, Earl drove on by,
seeking a nearby wide ravine and drove in deep.
The 4x4 sputtered and died,
now hidden from view.

Earl dug out his last smoke,
lit it off the lighter and leaned back,
kicking out the front windshield, his escape route,
since the doors were snow drift blocked shut.

As Earl crawled out the front,
he grabbed the red bandana.
Always wanted one, he thought,
trekking back to the double-wide.

Dead ends

Stale smoke, dirty dishes, a lit can of Sterno
greeted Earl inside the doublewide.
Before him, half reclined on a thin mattress,
blankets pulled to the chin, was his card-playing,
ranch hand buddy, Pete, the one who used to ride broncs.

Pete made the mistake of restarting his career
on a dare from a lady sporting great legs and green eyes.
His draw was a buckskin named "Dun Regret."
The ride proved unfortunate and short, with the bronc
making two crow hops and a fishtail out the gate.
Pete learned the hard way that reflexes,
and the glory days, were long gone.
His back was bad tweaked and his leg needed resetting.

Earl, upon hearing this news a few weeks back,
changed his own plans about giving
the Badland Circuit another go.
Instead, Earl began to mosey in the direction
of his friend in need, especially since he knew
his friend had a roof, and winter was here.

Hello, Earl said, *you look like a sight for sore eyes.*
"That and a penny" said the former bronc rider.
"I'm busted up, no good. I got to rest a spell.
But there's a bright side. A church lady
comes by, leaves a casserole every Friday noon.
Sometimes we get in a bit of a cheery chatter.
I think she thinks I'm a soul to be saved.
She's single, no ring, so easy to tell."

"Earl" said Pete, "stay a while, but do me
and you a favor, pay for some heat. Find a job."

Earl nodded and realized he needed the facilities.
Upon entering the small, dingy bathroom,
he spotted the culprit causing bone-chilling cold.
A two-foot squarish hole had been chopped through
the outside tin siding, through the inside wall
along the top of the bathtub.
Bending down and looking through,
Earl could see a dilapidated little corral outback.
Apparently, the previous occupant had given
his horse access to a water tank.
Earl tacked a piece of plywood over the gaping hole,
an improvement in a still cold trailer house.

Earl tried to be a skinner for a fur buyer.
He sat with a sharp knife, endured heat
blasted from propane forced air,
pulling off coyote hides, then stretching them
on wooden frames, hauling carcasses out to dump.
Each time he thought he was finished
with his pile of thawed 'yotes, in came another
frozen batch, hitting the concrete
like driftwood. *Yuck*, he told the boss,
too much, no more.

Then he tried being a lamber,
birthing ewes in the low-roofed winter sheds
of a big sheep man. Earl soon found out
sheep were IQ challenged and hard to move.
He never learned their language.
Bastard, he ended up calling each
and every one of the thousands
of bleating, blatting, stupid, stinking sheep,
as he picked off the ticks from his shirt
and underwear each night before sleep.

Almost made him go back to skinning.
Didn't matter, that season had come and gone.

Earl sure missed cows. He asked around.
All the outfits said they were full.
No place for a back-on-your-heels cowboy,
when there's plenty of younger ones to hire cheap.

Come spring, Earl gave a try delivering bee hives
to pastures of yellow clover fields.
Careful as he was, he got bee stung upon bee sting.
Bees were not so sweet.

Then Earl spent the summer stretch cutting up
old junk iron with an oxy torch, hard, hot work.
If hell had a taste, the acrid smoke
from burning slag must come close.
Topping off the negatives,
all his pants had burnt holes.

By late fall, Earl was done in.
Every job he tried looked like a dead end.
He felt he had knotted his end of the rope
and the knot was almighty frayed.

Besides, Pete, the former bronc rider,
had gotten on the mend.
The casserole Fridays drop offs
had progressed to three course meals
and a few rounds of three-player poker,
with Earl, in the beginning, catching
the first couple hands.
Then soon, the three became two.

Earl could take a hint.
The autumn wind got blowing,
tumble weeds were rolling.
Earl rolled out.

Earl makes a choice

AKA Merle one day found himself
reading a poster tacked to a bar's bulletin board.
After a coyote hunt, the American Legion Auxiliary
was hosting an "All You Can Eat Chili Feed - $2,"
which was all he had in loose change
sagging in his blue jeans.

Earl looked at the bar tap,
picturing foamy suds and a numbed state of mind,
then he looked down at his stomach
and admitted to being almighty hungry.

Making a decision setting the rest of his life
in motion, he opened the bar door,
making his way to the community hall
two doors down.

The bright, blinding sunshine hit him
as he took a dozen or so slow steps on the sidewalk.
Earl got his courage up, seeing the door
with a "Chili Feed - $2" poster taped on it,
and stepped into an entirely different world,
clean clothes, no rips, combed hair,
a buzz of cheerful conversation,
and women who looked like housewives
setting out the pickles, buns and chili,
almost like he had stepped into a church.
He lined up, plate in hand.

Ahead of him was a young man,
black hair, clean cut, polite as all get out
in a friendly sort of way. "Hey," the younger man said,
"I pulled you out of a snow bank last year.
I'm here for the coyote hunt. Small world, isn't it?"

Two chairs side-by-side
were all that was left to sit down.
Polite stranger and Earl both sat down.
This kid does look kinda familiar, thought Earl.

Earl proceeded to wolf down chili and chunks of bread.
Where're you from? he asked, curious-like.
"Back further east where the big auction barn is,"
said the polite stranger. Grew up on a ranch."
Oh, said Earl, grabbing another big spoonful.
"My uncle is the sheriff. Maybe you heard the name."

Earl paused in swallowing, a long, long pause.
His mind raced to a frightening revelation.
Haltingly, Earl asked,
By chance, what's your mom's name?
Polite stranger, smiling with loving pride, said,
"Sue Zann."

At that, Earl began to choke.
His face turned white, then red and on to blue,
kinda purple, too.
Tears flowed from his eyes. No one in the hall
seemed to know what to do.

Desperate, Earl got up and ran, stomach first,
into a corner of a table, knocking it over,
dishes, silverware, chili flew, hitting the floor,
and so did Earl, knocking himself out, too.
There he was gasping, a kaleidoscope of facial color.

Some were more concerned about the chili feed
being up-ended or folks leaving, but the polite stranger
knew what to do. He called 911.

Rambling on not taken

An ambulance came and loaded Earl up,
although by then he had come to and the purple
was back to red. He just wanted to find an exit.
But that polite stranger stayed by his side,
helping, preventing escape.

Down the road the ambulance went, wiggly-piggly,
since the roads were half ice. A driver up front,
a paramedic in the back, Earl strapped down on a bench,
thinking when they get to the hospital,
he'd get out and make a run. He was OK enough.
Besides, he had no money, no insurance.

Around a curve, over a hill, into a dip,
with a cow dead-centered on the road, a side-ways skip,
around and around, lights flashing, the white ambulance
tumbled down the ditch, through a fence,
hitting a big rock, stopping, creaking,
smelling of spilled gas.

Earl came to, his butt in a snow drift, wet and cold,
sitting on the shoulder of the ice-covered road.
Square in front of him was the double door
of the ambulance, wide open to the sky.
Nobody stirring inside.

Down the ditch, a hundred yards off,
a big black cow contentedly ambled along,
munching frozen grass, unconcerned
with her part in this chain of events.

The road stretched each way endlessly to the horizon,
sweet freedom of the horizon – get on the road,
amble off, go forever, anyplace, anywhere.

Such a thought, thought Earl.
Then he spotted a thin whisp of smoke
rising from the wreck. *Oh my*, thought Earl.
Not good.

Two trips down the ditch, two back up,
dragging the mumbling driver
and unconscious paramedic away to safety,
before, with a woof of smoke
and a blam of fire, the whole kit of the ambulance
went kaboodle, up in flames.

Coming from further up the highway,
Earl could see blue, red, white lights flashing.
Oh my, my, here comes the law.
Earl was just too exhausted, too tired to run.
In all practicality, where?

The cop asked, "What's your name?"
Earl, without thinking, said, *Earl.*

Hero Earl

Whether he wanted or not, Earl had a bed
for the night in the hospital.

The next morning a TV crew was in his room,
interviewing him on his heroics,
saved two men from fiery deaths,
instead of being saved by them.
Earl's face made headlines.
Irony makes news.

A bit groggy from some pain-killer drugs,
he let slip out his full God-given legal name,
which is how his hospital bill came to be paid
as he was checking out the next day.

Polite stranger signing papers at the desk
looked up and said, "How are you feeling, Earl?
Or is it Ok if I start calling you Dad?"

Well, you know, even after twenty years
or so, it's still a shock when the day dawns
and the jig is up.

All Earl could think of to say, with a gulp,
Hi there, son?! What's your...ahh...name?
"Mike is my given, but for some reason,
my friends call me Sue, after my mother."

Yeah, about that, Mike...ahh...Sue...
how is your mother?

"Doing quite well, owns the ranch,
Granddad died a while back.
Mom never married, only told me
of a magical night
with a 'Knight of the Prairie' named Earl.
Always wondered what she said
that made him disappear.
Mom asked around, even went to the stockyards,
but no one knew where you were.
Just like that, gone.
Had her wondering if Granddad
had something to do with it."

There are times in a man's life
when he's gotta think of his prospects.
It took Earl about three seconds
to think it through.

Tender mercies

That is how Earl, hat in hand,
came to be standing
on the doorstep of the biggest ranch house
he'd ever seen, gazing hopefully
upon a mighty fine-looking lady
with grey speckled,
no longer quite as long black hair, saying,
Hi! I'm Earl.

There was bit of silence and a look up and down.
Then, she smiled.

It's amazing what a few trips
to the dentist can do,
plus, a haircut, shave and brand-new clothes,
to remake a man.

Now and again, Earl heads off to the local bar,
buys a round for all the cowboy tramps
sitting outside on the wooden benches,
bids them good luck and leaves.

He heads up to the auction barn,
takes a seat in a cushioned chair,
sells a few head, buys a few head,
pays, or picks up a check.

Earl always bee-lines it back to Sue Zann
who, after all these years,
never forgot about him,
and believed.

Bruce Roseland
Poet Laureate of South Dakota

Bruce Roseland is the 8th Poet Laureate of South Dakota (2023-2027). Roseland refers to himself as a prairie poet. His poetry describes people, work and nature in modern rural life. Roseland's poems often reveal the sacred in relationships between the land, the life it supports and those who are its stewards. His recent work describes the need to conserve native grasslands. Roseland believes poems are little stories about what matters to us, and that these stories connect us, make it possible for us to see each other. His goal as Poet Laureate is to make poetry accessible, to encourage folks from all walks of life to write, read their poetry publicly and share their work with other writers and their communities.

Roseland is the author of eight books of free verse poetry and has won four national awards, including *The Last Buffalo* (2006), 2007 Wrangler Award; *A Prairie Prayer* (2008), 2009 Will Rogers

Medallion; *Church of the Holy Sunrise* (2012); *Song for My Mother* (2014); *Gift of Moments* (2016); *Cowman* (2018), 2019 Will Rogers Medallion; *Heart of the Prairie* (2021) 2022 Will Rogers Medallion; and *Earl's Own Dakota Odyssey, A West River Story* (2024). Roseland received a M.A. in Sociology, 1980, from the University of North Dakota. He is President Emeritus of SD State Poetry Society and a South Dakota Humanities Scholar.

Roseland is a fourth-generation cattleman who grew up on a ranch in north central South Dakota. He still works his family ranch outside of Seneca, South Dakota, but also enjoys spending time in his Black Hills Spearfish home when cows and crops permit.

Bruce Roseland's books are available on Amazon.

Made in the USA
Middletown, DE
26 July 2024

57937663R00050